THIS BOOK
BELONGS TO

....

....

KNOCK, KNOCK.

WHO'S THERE?

WITCH.

WITCH WHO?

WITCH IS LOOKING
FOR HER BLACK CAT.

KNOCK KNOCK.

WHO'S THERE?
BEN.

BEN WHO?

BEN WAITING FOR A
FULL MOON.

KNOCK, KNOCK.

WHO'S THERE?

LUKE.

LUKE WHO?

LUKE AT THE BIG SPIDER ON YOUR ARM!

Q: WHAT DOES A SPIDER DO WHEN HE GETS ANGRY?

A: HE GOES UP THE WALL!

Q:WHAT DID THE SPIDER SAY TO THE FLY ON HALLOWEEN?

A:THE WEB IS THE TRICK AND YOU ARE THE TREAT

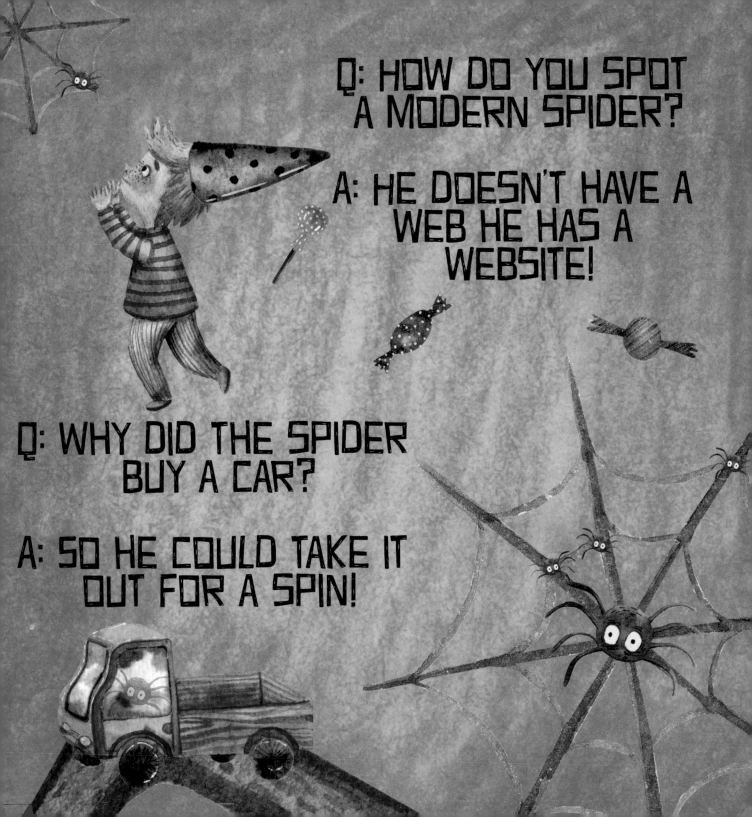

Q: HOW DO YOU SPOT A MODERN SPIDER?

A: HE DOESN'T HAVE A WEB HE HAS A WEBSITE!

Q: WHY DID THE SPIDER BUY A CAR?

A: SO HE COULD TAKE IT OUT FOR A SPIN!

KNOCK, KNOCK.

WHO'S THERE?

PHILLIP.

PHILLIP WHO?

PHILLIP MY BAG
WITH HALLOWEEN
CANDY PLEASE.

KNOCK, KNOCK.

WHO'S THERE?

WITCHES.

WITCHES WHO?

WITCHES THE WAY
TO THE HAUNTED
HOUSE.

KNOCK, KNOCK

WHO'S THERE?

BOO!

BOO WHO?

DON'T CRY! I WAS
JUST KIDDING.

Q: WHAT IS A WITCH'S FAVORITE SUBJECT IN SCHOOL?

A: SPELLING

Q: WHAT DO WITCHES GET AT HOTELS?

A: BROOM SERVICE

Q: WHAT DO YOU CALL TWO WITCHES LIVING TOGETHER?

A: BROOMMATES.

Q: WHAT DO WITCHES USE IN THEIR HAIR?

A: SCARE-SPRAY

Q: WHAT DO GHOSTS
EAT FOR DINNER?

A: SPOOKGETTI

Q: WHAT KIND OF GUM
DO GHOSTS CHEW?

A: BOO BOO GUM.

Q: WHAT KIND OF TIE DOES A GHOST WEAR TO A PARTY?

A: A BOO-TIE.

Q: WHAT IS A GHOST'S FAVORITE FOOD?

A: HAMBOOGERS

KNOCK KNOCK!

WHO'S THERE?

THE EARL.

THE EARL WHO?

THE EARL-Y BIRD
GETS THE BEST
HALLOWEEN CANDY!

KNOCK KNOCK!

WHO'S THERE?

DISGUISE.

DISGUISE WHO?

DISGUISE DRESSED UP LIKE A CRAZY WIZARD FOR HALLOWEEN!

Q: WHAT IS A BLACK CAT'S FAVORITE COLOR?

A: PURRRRRRR-PLE!

Q: WHY ARE BLACK CATS SUCH GOOD SINGERS?

A: THEY'RE VERY MEWSICAL!

Q: WHAT IS A BLACK CAT'S FAVOURITE SUBJECT IN SCHOOL?

A: HISSTORY!

Q: WHAT IS A BLACK CAT'S FAVOURITE DESSERT?

A: MICE PUDDING!

Q: WHAT DO YOU CALL AN
ATHLETIC PUMPKIN?

A: A JOCK O' LANTERN.

Q: WHO IS THE
LEADER OF ALL
PUMPKINS?

A: THE
PUMPKING

KNOCK KNOCK.
WHO'S THERE?
PUMPKIN.
PUMPKIN WHO?
KNOCK KNOCK.
WHO'S THERE?
PUMPKIN.
PUMPKIN WHO?
KNOCK KNOCK.
WHO'S THERE?
PUMPKIN.
PUMPKIN WHO?
KNOCK KNOCK.
WHO'S THERE?
ORANGE.
ORANGE WHO?
ORANGE YOU GLAD I DIDN'T SAY PUMPKIN AGAIN?

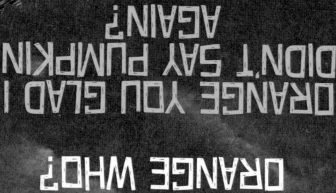

If you have enjoyed this book, we ask you kindly to please leave a review on Amazon. It has a significant impact on small businesses like us. Thank you so much!